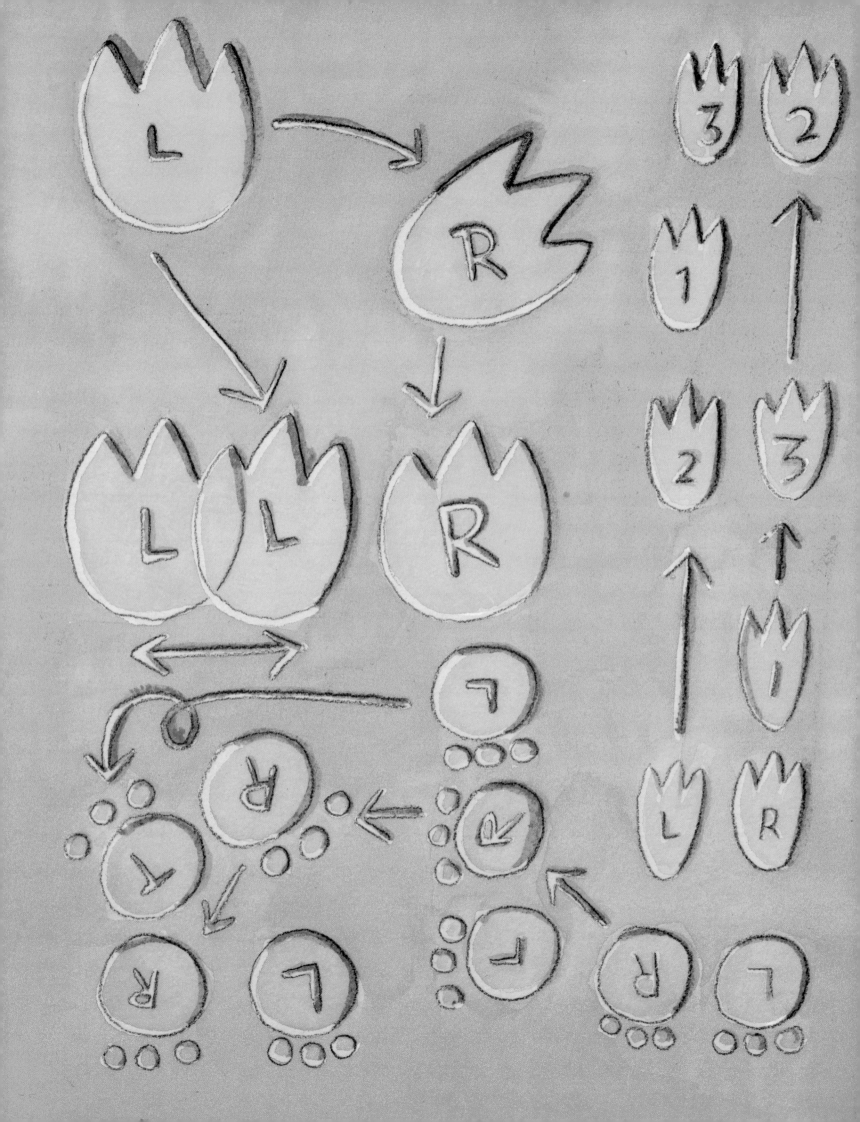

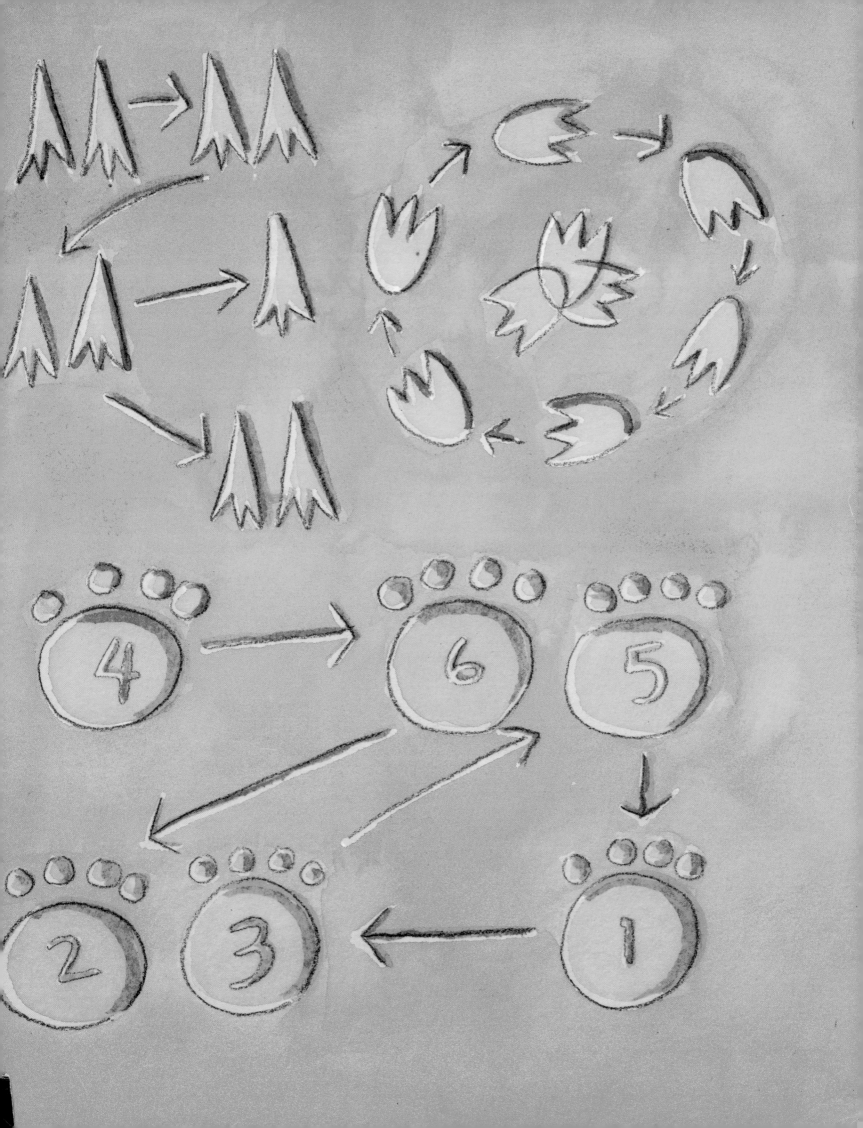

For Alex and Sam, with love
– C. D. S.

To Sarah, Timmy, Allison, Charlie, and Nancy
– S. N.

ISBN 0-590-03235-6

Text copyright © 1997 by Carol Diggory Shields.
Illustrations copyright © 1997 by Scott Nash.
All rights reserved.
Published by Scholastic Inc.,
555 Broadway, New York, NY 10012,
by arrangement with Candlewick Press.
SCHOLASTIC and associated logos are trademarks and/or
registered trademarks of Scholastic Inc.

12 11 10 9 8 7 6 5 4 3 2 1   8 9/9 0 1 2 3/0

Printed in the U.S.A.   08

First Scholastic printing, April 1998

This book was typeset in Cafeteria Bold.
The pictures were done in watercolor and pencil.

Saturday Night at the Dinosaur STOMP

Carol Diggory Shields

illustrated by Scott Nash

SCHOLASTIC INC.
New York Toronto London Auckland Sydney

Word went out 'cross the prehistoric slime:
"Hey, dinosaurs, it's rock 'n' roll time!
Slick back your scales and get ready to romp

On Saturday night at the **Dinosaur Stomp!**"

By the lava beds and the tar pit shore,
On the mountain top and the rain forest floor,

Dinosaurs scrubbed their necks and nails.
They brushed their teeth and curled their tails.

Then – ready, set, go – they trampled and tromped,

Making dinosaur tracks for the Dinosaur Stomp.

Plesiosaurus paddled up with a splash

Protoceratops brought along her eggs

A batch of bouncing babies followed Mama Maiasaur

A pterodactyl family flew in for the bash.

Diplodocus plodded on big fat legs.

he last time she counted, she had twenty-four.

The old ones gathered in a gossiping bunch,
Sitting and sipping sweet Swampwater Punch.

Dinosaurs giggled and shuffled and stared,
Ready to party, but a little bit scared.

Then Iguanodon shouted, "One, *two,* three!"
Started up the band by waving a tree.

Brachio-, Super-, and Ultrasaurus
Sang, "Doo-bop-a-loo-bop," all in a chorus.
Ankylosaurus drummed on his hard-shelled back,
Boomalacka boomalacka! Whack! Whack!
Whack!

Pentaceratops stood up to perform
And blasted a tune on his favorite horn.

They played in rhythm, they sang in rhyme,
Dinosaur music in dinosaur time!

Duckbill thought he'd take a chance:
Asked Allosaurus if she'd like to dance.

Tarchia winked at a stegosaur she liked.
They danced together, spike to spike.

The Triassic Twist and the Brontosaurus Bump,
The Raptor Rap and Jurassic Jump.

Tyrannosaurus Rex led a conga line.
Carnosaurs capered close behind.
They rocked and rolled, they twirled and tromped.
There never was a party like the **Dinosaur Stomp.**

The nighttime sky began to glow.
Volcanoes put on a fireworks show.
The ground was rocking – it started to shake.
Those dinosaurs danced up the first earthquake!

The party went on – it was so outrageous,

They stayed up well past the late Cretaceous.

When the Cenozoic dawned they were tired and beat.
They yawned big yawns and put up their feet.

And they're *still* asleep, snoring deep in the swamp.
But they'll be back . . . next **Dinosaur Stomp!**

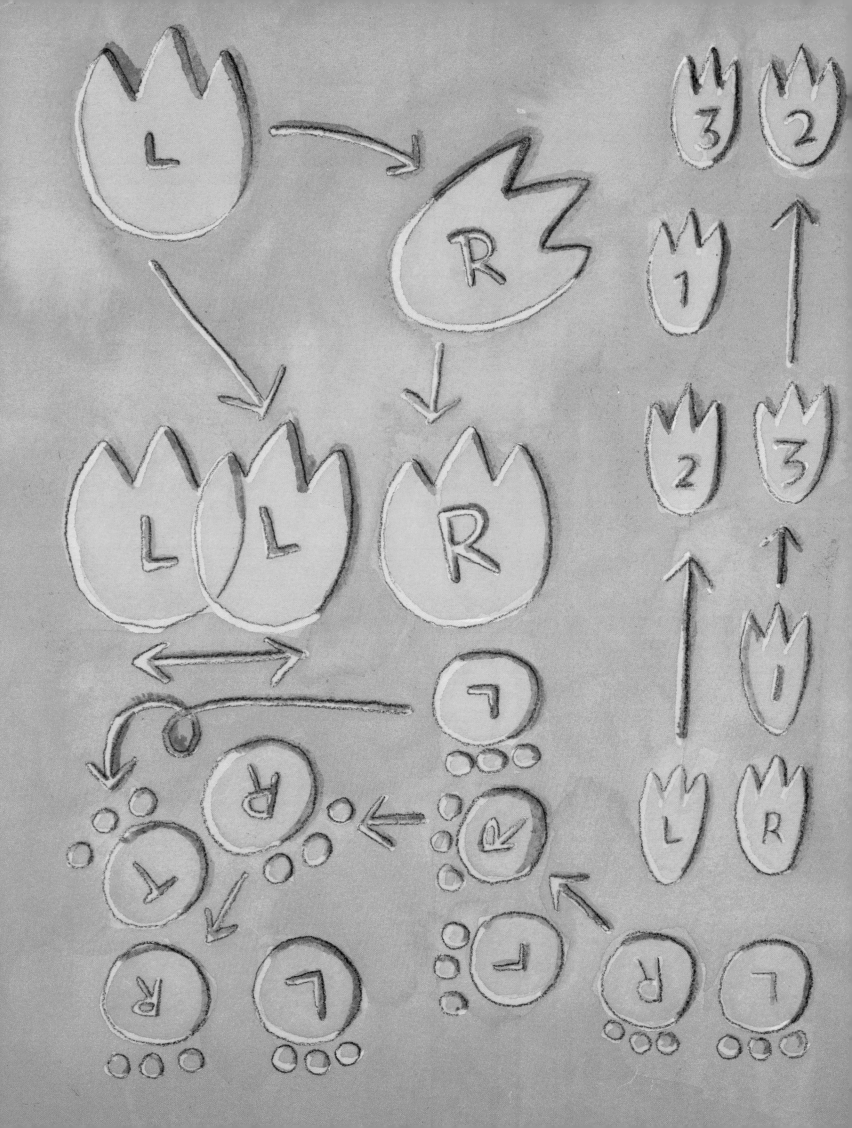

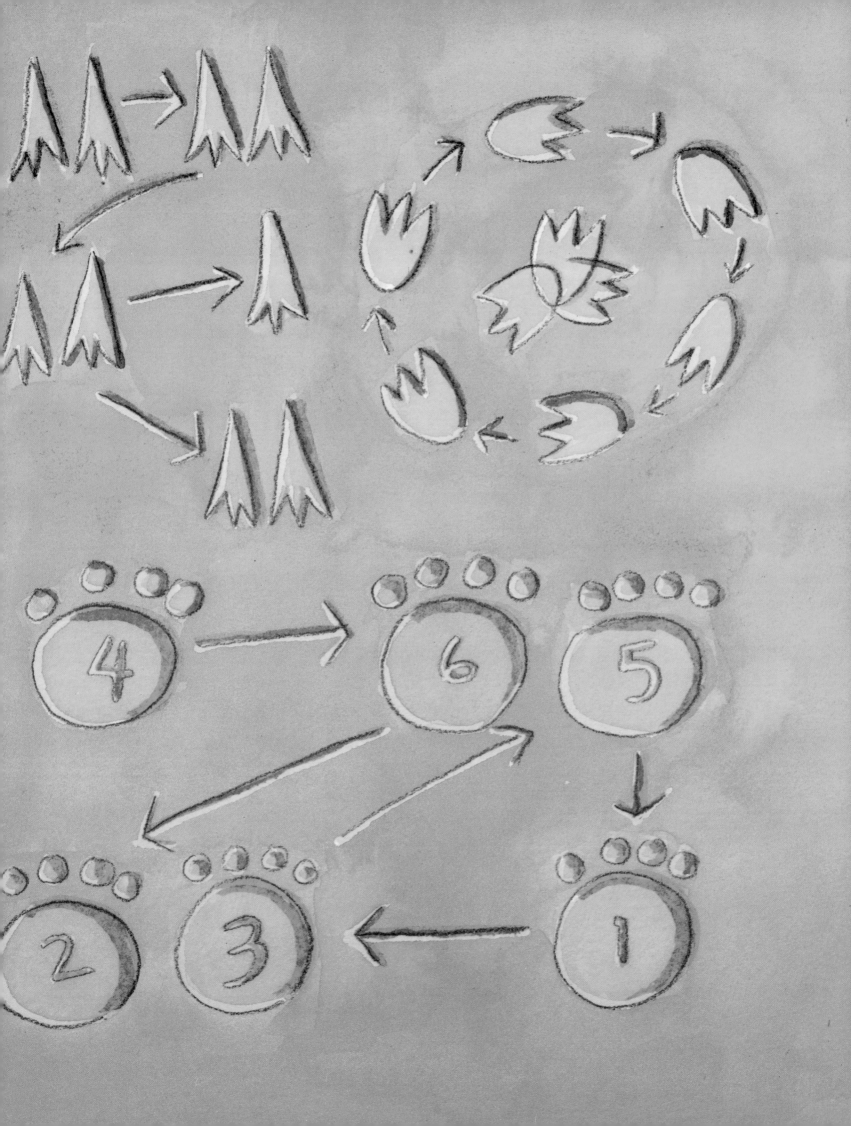